SAFE AND SECURE IN ATROPIA
by Rainbow Albrecht

Copyright 2014 Rainbow Albrecht
Amazon Edition

"Those who would give up essential Liberty, to purchase a little temporary Safety, deserve neither Liberty nor Safety."
- Benjamin Franklin

Dedicated to Captain Gatso of MAD, and all others who take direct action to oppose the slow encroachment against liberty.

The oppressive summer heat had died down into warmth that would almost be tolerable if not for the humidity. In the emphatically nice suburban community of Atropia, the evening's quiet was punctuated only by the chirping of crickets and the whirring of air conditioners. That is, until the beating of helicopter blades filled the air. A small drone flew down the streets. Sonar chirps meticulously probed the terrain as a laser swept close to the ground. The tips of a few blades of grass glowed in the red beam. When the drone acquired its target, it radioed the location to headquarters.

Within minutes, four squad cars of heavily-armed police rushed down the street - stealthily, without sirens or lights - and converged on one of the houses. The officers got out and assembled at the door. Orders were whispered and a battering ram was brought to the front. On a count of three, wood splintered and the door burst inward. The police rushed into the house. One of the officers kicked open the door to the main bedroom. He ran in and pointed his service revolver at a young couple in bed. "Got 'em!" he shouted.

The squad leader, a young kid barely out of the academy, ran into the bedroom. He shouted an order at the others to keep searching.

The man in bed said, "We didn't do anything. You must have the wrong house. And can't you see we're trying to have a private moment?" His girlfriend glared at the cops indignantly and pulled the sheets up higher. Still, she was glad she didn't have time to reach for the pistol in the drawer; things could have gone very badly.

"We hear that one all the time. I assure, you, efficiency is our greatest asset, thanks to The Computer. You're Vinnie Ferretti, and according to your dossier, that's your paramour Julie."

"What's this all about? I'm going to be pretty upset if someone is pulling a prank on us."

"We're here to cite you for criminal neglect." He pulled out a pad of forms and started writing a ticket. "Your lawn was found to be above the statutory limit."

"I mowed it on Monday, for crying out loud!"

"It was above the limit by a quarter of an inch. The law's the law. Since this is a first offense, the ticket will only be $165 during the grace period. You can either pay it, or if you choose to contest it, you have the right to adjudicate it before the judge."

"What? You've got to be kidding me!"

Julie said, "This is absurd. You could've just come at a normal time of day and knocked. And who's going to pay for the doors?"

The squad leader gave her a funny look. "Not us, that's for sure. Keeping yards orderly is very serious business. I wouldn't be complaining too much if I were you; there's talk in City Council that they should be cracking down on lawn crimes even harder and raise it to a Class B misdemeanor."

"The same as drunk driving?"

"You got it, sweetheart." He ripped the ticket off the pad and handed it to Vinnie, and handily also proffered a pen. "Here's your Statement Of Infraction. Sign this."

"Like hell I'm signing that!"

"Your choice. You're the owner of record, so you either sign it, or we put you in handcuffs and give you a free ride downtown. Then you will be booked and later arraigned. Fortunately for you, bond is usually no more than $500."

"Fine," growled Vinnie. He scrawled his signature on the Statement Of Infraction and handed back the top copy.

Two more cops came into the room, one holding a baggie with a green herb in it. "All clear. But look at what we found."

The squad leader laughed. "Well, well, well!"

Julie gave them a sour look. "That's oregano. My mother grew it in her garden."

"I'm going to do you a very big favor today. We'll send it into the lab for a chemical assay, and if you're telling the truth, we'll bill you for the test and that'll be the end of that. But if you're lying, then we'll be back."

Vinnie said, "I know the law. You can't just bust down our door and toss the house."

"Actually, we can tear out the drywall if we feel like it." The squad leader handed him a warrant. "The standard document covers everything."

"You call this a search warrant? This is a boilerplate form, and I bet it was signed with an autopen."

"Actually, you're right. But it's still valid. The judge pre-authorized its use in any lawn neglect crimes. The judicial authority to issue warrants has been delegated to The Computer. No need to wake up the judge for that."

"But it's okay to disturb us in bed over bullshit? And what about probable cause?"

"If you persist in vulgar language, I'll be quite happy to take you in for disorderly conduct. The standard search warrant form includes everything in case there are any ancillary crimes."

The cop who found the baggie said, "Even if not for the warrant, it wouldn't hold up to a probable cause challenge. We were searching for occupants, and that was in plain sight, in the spice rack in the back of the pantry. If you want to debate legal theory, then pay the court fee and talk to the judge. To do so, you will need to make out a $150 money order payable to the City of Atropia for the court fee. The details are all on the back of the Statement Of Infraction."

"This is, uh, rubbish!"

The squad leader warned him, "If you persist in arguing, we can take your paramour downtown for marijuana possession; she admitted it's hers. The lab results get back within two weeks. Usually."

A beefy cop, his hair mostly gray, grabbed the baggie and sniffed the contents. "It's oregano, for crying out loud. Haven't you kids ever had a real pizza? You should try it some time."

The squad leader glared at him. "Have you forgotten who's in charge here?"

"You can take your rank and cram it. This has gone far enough. If I need to bend you over my knee and give you a good paddling, I will. Let's get out of here." They had a brief staredown. The older man won.

City Hall was an old building made of limestone blocks, though several additions had been constructed in modern style, which really didn't fit in architecturally with the original structure. And this certainly included the opulent entrance. The rococo ironwork sign above the front gate read, "*Labor Facit Liber*".

They followed the primrose-lined sidewalk to the door and entered.

Vinnie and Julie took a number and waited interminably on benches that were so uncomfortable that they could have doubled as medieval torture instruments. The easy listening music was suitable for use in enhanced interrogations, though of questionable legality according to the Geneva Conventions. As they waited in the lobby, they read with scant interest the story written on a mural of how Atropia had been founded in 1851 by a group of Danish immigrants from Jante. The settlers of old built a small town by a creek that had a peculiar wheel-shaped stone in the middle. The community grew when the railroad was built through it, and later, an interstate highway. In recent times, it became an important edge city and attracted some big businesses. When they were done reading the wall, they gazed at the intricate parquet patterns in the granite floor. It featured an enormous inscription inlaid in rose quartz, *"Non Potestis Pugnare Civitatem Prætorium"*.

When their number finally came up, they went to the desk and showed their Statement Of

Infraction. The receptionist directed them down the hall, second door on the right. On the way, they got a refreshing drink from a water fountain. It tasted like ditch water, which is why many houses in the area had expensive filtration systems.

They came to the department, marked "City of Atropia Lawn Gestapo", and entered. The front desk was adorned with a nameplate for Ms. Roberts. The munchkin occupying the seat behind the desk was staring at a computer screen and moving the mouse quite a bit. After five minutes passed without so much as an acknowledging look, Vinnie walked to the side. There was a framed motivational poster that, in Pyongyang, would have fit right in if it were translated into Korean. In the poster's reflection, he could see that Ms. Roberts was playing solitaire. He walked back and chimed the bell on the desk. Summoned properly, the munchkin sprang into life.

"What do you want?"

Julie said, "We got some kind of ticket about our yard." She held up the Statement Of Infraction.

"You're within the grace period, so that will be $165."

"Well, actually, we wanted to talk to someone in charge about it."

Ms. Roberts gave her a quizzical look. "You want to do *what*?"

Vinnie said, "We would like to speak with someone in charge. Who's the head of this outfit?"

She sighed. "Ms. Beria is in an all-day meeting. Tomorrow too. And she doesn't liaise with the general public."

"Is there someone else who, you know, does?"

She started drumming her fingers. "Well, there's Mr. Bathory. He had an appointment for two minutes ago, but it got cancelled. He's the assistant secretary for the ROFLCOPTER program."

"The *what*?"

"Residential Over-Flight Lawn Compliance Observation Project Telemetric Enforcement Robot. You know, the drone that goes through the streets every week to make sure that yards are all in order. You should be glad that the City of Atropia is performing this valuable service to the public in order to keep standards maintained and property values high."

"Oh, is that the contraption that ratted me out for the 'lawn crime'? The first time I saw it from the bedroom window, I thought I was having a nightmare. Anyway, sure, we'll see Mr. Bathory."

The munchkin sighed, reluctantly minimized the card game, and brought up an ungainly interface for The Computer. The browser that it displayed on crashed and had to be started again. The second time went better. After a few clicks, she announced, "Sorry, the Computer won't let me schedule an appointment after the time slot has begun."

Julie asked, "Could you just show us to his desk?"

"Not without scheduling an appointment in The Computer."

Vinnie exclaimed, "This is absurd!"

"Lower your voice, mister! Normally I'd let you in, but it's Policy."

"How does it feel, servitude to software?"

"What do you mean?"

"Think of all those science fiction stories where the machines rise up and conquer humanity. We can't stop them because they're powerful, they have no fear, they feel no pain, and they're nearly indestructible. This was the nightmare scenario from *Rossum's Universal Robots* all the way up to the *Terminator* movies. But the way the future really turned out is that you bureaucrats let yourselves be controlled by some database application."

She said curtly, "We have to do what The Computer says; it's Policy."

"You have the God-given gifts of free will and discretion, something that no machine will ever have. Free your mind!"

"Around here, we Trust The System."

He sighed. "*Domo arigato*, Ms. Roboto. Any appointments tomorrow? We want to get this thing resolved."

"Everyone's booked up. And off the record, I can assure you that it'll just be a waste of time. You're better off seeing the judge if that's how you feel about it."

"Yeah, but that involves more payola, and the fine print says the court fee doesn't apply to the ticket if we lose the case. Look, can't you just give me a break? This is the first time."

"Early on, They decided that there will be no waivers or exceptions, and the ROFLCOPTER program is here to stay." Helpfully, she warned, "The grace period ends in five minutes when the office closes. Then the fine goes up to $215."

Vinnie replied, "Fine, whatever, we'll pay. Do you take American Express?"

"No. Only cash, certified checks, postal money orders, and Yemeni *hawala* transfers."

Fortunately, between them they had nine $20 bills. The munchkin took the cash and handed back a receipt.

"Where's the change?"

"Change?"

"There should be fifteen bucks change. Hey, I'm not judging; not everyone is good with arithmetic. I bet there's a calculator feature on your computer. Or I could show you how to figure it on a spreadsheet."

"Well, They don't let us make change. It's Policy."

They left the building just as the guard was kicking out everyone on the benches who had drawn numbers a few higher than they had. When they got to the car, they saw a yellow slip tucked under the windshield wiper. Vinnie grabbed it. "What the hell?" He read the ticket. "Closer than three inches to the curb?" He took a closer look. "I say it's just right."

Julie got a tape measure from her purse. "Three and a half inches. Want to take a picture?"

"Good luck proving it; They will just say we moved the car."

She looked at the ticket. "This says we have to drop by some church to pay it, and we can't mail it in. That's weird. I wonder why?"

On Sunday morning, Vinnie and Julie exited the freeway and passed through a toll booth that, thanks to space age technology, scanned the transponder stuck to the car's windshield and then deducted his account.

Vinnie grumbled, "A couple of years ago, they didn't have these. Whoever thought of taking a highway that had been around for decades and sticking a bunch of toll booths on it?"

Julie replied, "Someone very creative about siphoning money from the public's pockets, that's for sure! It's hard to get anywhere lately without getting dinged on the road, both ways. But what really gets me is that when I went to the mall the other day, I found that they had put in pay toilets."

"This is nuts. I haven't seen a pay toilet since I was a kid in New Jersey."

"Good thing I had some change that day. I doubt any of it's going to go to cleaning up all the graffiti tagging, or hiring a second rent-a-cop, one who actually does something. I never go there at night any more. What good are all those cameras in the parking lot if they don't prevent the muggings?"

They came up to the church, such as it was. There were no structures other than several rows of carports arranged in a semicircular fashion. Already people had started to show up. Vinnie parked the car under one of them.

An usher rushed up promptly. "Excuse me, but this space is reserved. Unless you have an authorized hang tag, you have to use one of the rows further back. Would you like to apply for a reserved space?"

"Uh, thanks but no thanks."

"And one other thing, you have to park precisely straight here. The Parkifex Maximus is very strict about that."

"Okay, whatever." He started the car again, got into a row further back, and made sure to pull it in precisely. He got out and asked the usher, with a mild note of irritation, "Is this straight enough for you?"

"Much better. It is right and meet to park properly, as the path to righteousness is along the straight and narrow."

"Whatever. Look, I'm just here to pay a ticket. Who am I supposed to see about that? Isn't there an office somewhere?"

"It will be right after the sermon. Services should start before long." They waited with little patience as dozens of other parishioners pulled into their parking spaces.

In ten minutes, a tow truck with lots of shiny chrome - or perhaps silver plating - pulled in and came to rest precisely at the focus of the semicircle. As he did so, everyone respectfully shut off their engines. Vinnie did so too, so as not to stick out. He rolled down the windows and the sweltering warm air enveloped them.

The heat was oppressive even under the shade of the carport.

A man got out of the tow truck, dressed in a vestment that was a compromise between mechanic's overalls and an Eastern Orthodox priest's cassock. He welcomed the congregation.

"Greetings, Holy Father," replied everyone present, except Vinnie and Julie. After that, he preached one of the most boring sermons ever delivered in the English language. It was something to do with whether faith was of the nature of concrete or asphalt. The Parkifex Maximus never got around to saying which one it was, but nobody cared one way or another. Fortunately, it was only ten minutes long, though it seemed like an amusement park version of Purgatory.

Then the procession began. Beginning with the front row, passengers got out of the cars and lined up in front of a parking meter by the pickup. Vinnie watched the first communicant, an elderly lady dressed in her Sunday's finest. She stood before the parking meter, made the sign of the 'P' in the air, then knelt down. She fed a quarter into the meter and turned the knob. She bowed her head reverently and rose.

Vinnie said quietly, "What kind of stupid ritual is this?" He wiped sweat from his brow and unsuccessfully tried to shoo a mosquito out of the car.

"Well, different strokes for different folks, I suppose."

The Parkifex Maximus called out, "Are there any repentant souls with tickets? Step ye forth that ye may receive absolution."

Julie said, "I think he means you."

Vinnie got out and jogged forward on the sun-baked pavement toward the tow truck, eager to get done with this as soon as possible. Others started to line up behind him.

The Parkifex Maximus took the citation from him and announced, "We have a sinner here today who is eager to do penance and cleanse his soul. Thou, Vincent Ferretti, art guilty of the transgression of…" He glanced at the ticket again, "Parking too close to the curb. Behold, the Legiscripture hath deemed that thy tires may only tarry within 3-18 inches of the curb. It is written; thus saith the Law."

"Yeah, I read that on the ticket. Look, can I just pay this? Without all the mummery?"

"Thou canst not receive absolution without a contrite and repentant heart!"

"Uh, I'm sorry, I'm just not used to any of this. You see, I'm Catholic, and we do the confession thing in a box and then say prayers, so all this is new. But, I'm, uh, totally repentant. *Mea culpa. Mea maxima culpa.*" He thought of pounding on his chest, then decided he wasn't really feeling up to it.

"Then thou shalt give unto Caesar."

Vinnie opened his wallet and pulled out the plunder. He had made sure ahead of time that he had the exact amount. He fed the bills into a golden lock box at the feet of the Parkifex Maximus. He got up and headed toward his car.

"Wait! Thou shalt make obeisance to the parking meter! Thou canst not be shriven otherwise!"

He got in place behind the long line of worshipers who were waiting to kneel at the meter and feed quarters to their idol. "Uh, does anyone have change for a fiver?"

Vinnie was fuming as he drove home. "I can't believe this! Whoever thought of making a religion about parking?"

"Football is a religion here too."

"Well, at least that's fun to watch. Even the beer commercials are a little entertaining."

"Look out! Yellow light!" They heard the screeching of tires from the cars behind them. Then cars further back leaned on their brakes, and barely avoided colliding with the cars forced to make a hard stop.

But it was too late. They were already in the intersection. Just as the car was exiting, an array of strobe lights went off, though it wasn't necessary in the bright daylight. When the bank of cameras was installed, They reduced the timing of the yellow light from five seconds to three, for obvious reasons.

Vinnie said some choice words.

"I think the car that was next to us got tagged. They were a foot or two back. We might be safe. Maybe."

"Poor guy. I guess we'll find out soon enough if I'm busted too. I wonder if They'll send a squad of shock troops this time?"

They made a right turn and came to the entrance to their gated community. The twelve foot high walls around the road-facing part of it were made of decorative brickwork. But they were topped with triple concertina wire which detracted from the aesthetics. After all, the Berlin Wall modestly featured just a tube-like design at the top to prevent escapees from getting a handhold. But one thing the structures had in common was the amount of graffiti, the difference being that the West Germans had much better artistic ability.

Vinnie activated a remote control, and the first portcullis creaked upward. Under the watchful eyes of an impressive array of cameras, the car rolled through. Then the gate behind them clanked shut and the second gate rose. "Every time I go through here, I get nervous that the exit gate will malfunction."

Julie said, "All this security isn't doing a very good job of keeping us safe. There've been three burglaries in the neighborhood since we got here. Do you think they're coming through that hole in the fence by the park that They never fix?"

"Could be. But maybe not. The fact is, burglars all live somewhere too. Nobody ever thinks of that one."

The couple arrived at home. Vinnie got the mail. He stood by the recycle box and, one at a time, dropped in all the flyers that constituted most of their correspondence. "Spam, spam, spam. Hey, what's this?"

Julie took the letter and tore it open. "It's from the Homeowner's Association." She scanned down the page. "The Board of Directors voted to increase fees by $25 a month."

"And speaking of thieves! Three hundred bucks more a year? We've only been here a couple months! Is this like a housewarming gift or something? I'm beginning to regret moving to this place."

"It could be worse. I hear the HOA fees in the Dragonwyck development are double what we're paying. I'm not sure why. It's not like they have a pool or anything, or even a garden. Neither do we, for that matter. I wonder where it all goes?"

"It's to pay the panel of 80 year old ladies who tell you that you're not allowed to paint your own house. Fortunately, the grannies in our HOA don't charge as much as the ones in Dragonwyck. Yet."

"Maybe we should go to the next meeting and tell them what we think."

He laughed. "That dog and pony show? The first time we were there, I decided it would be my last. The whole experience reminded me of something Bismarck said."

"Really? What was that?"

"In English, it goes: 'Not through speeches or majority decisions will the great questions of the time be decided… rather through iron and blood.'"

In the pre-dawn hours, the ROFLCOPTER began its weekly cruise through the streets of Atropia. First it came to the edge of an old neighborhood. Vinnie hid behind a thick hedge of bushes, biding his time. He undid the fasteners on a long case. It was time for payback.

Just as the drone started to pass by, he pointed a tube through an opening in the bushes. He pulled the triggering lever. Fire roared from the back of the tube as a rocket shot forward on a trail of red flame. The warhead struck the ROFLCOPTER in midair, destroying it in a terrific explosion. The wreckage hit the pavement and skidded into a ditch.

Vinnie breathed a sigh of relief. He put the launch tube back in the case and closed it. In the grand scheme of things, it was but a small blow against petty despotism. But even if it was barely more than a symbolic gesture, delivering it satisfied his soul like little else had lately.

Even so, his nerves were on edge. He would have to backtrack, through areas where there were no cameras (that he knew about, anyway), then through the break in the fence, and finally back to his house. He slung the case over his back, picked up his bicycle, and turned around to leave.

There was someone standing at the curb. It was the older police officer from when his house was raided for the 'lawn crime' two weeks ago. He said slowly, "Son, you just cost the city a small fortune."

A chill went through Vinnie's body, as if his blood turned to ice. Briefly he thought of fleeing, but he would be a sitting duck in the park across the street. He dropped the bicycle, put down the case, and raised his hands. He wondered how many years in prison he was going to get.

The cop walked up. "At ease, soldier. I must say, you're a pretty good shot."

"You're… not going to arrest me?"

He laughed. "Hell no! If I was going to bust you, I already would've. You see, I live just down the street." He pointed to a house with a flagpole in the front yard. "I'm not working graveyard this week, so I went out for a jog before it gets hotter than hell. You gave me the most entertainment I've had in years. I'm not here, and neither are you; deal? Say, what kind of rocket is that?"

"It's sort of a reproduction of a late-model Panzerfaust. I'm a machinist, you see. And I have a knack for chemistry."

"It wasn't like this, when I signed on in '83. The Force was much smaller, and we only busted real criminals, which we did quite well. But things changed. We started running radar all the time. Personally, I don't give a tin-plated crap if someone is going a little over the limit, but speed traps are big business. I'm happy to pull over drivers who've got a bug up their ass, but it's hard to spot things like lane encroachments and tailgating when you're hiding behind the bushes watching a radar gun. These days, we issue citations about all sorts of bullshit having nothing to do with public safety. And as for cameras, they started popping up like toadstools. Used to be only banks had them. Finally, these damn drone overflights." He pointed to the smoldering wreck of the ROFLCOPTER.

"Sam Francis was a brilliant commentator who described 'anarcho-tyranny'. The government talks tough about cracking down on crime, but they only care about *appearing* to do something. So it's all about security theater, expanding power and control, domestic spying, selectively harassing so-called extremists, pumping up budgets, and creatively fleecing honest citizens. They could take effective action, but we only get empty gestures and a pile of new laws that don't do much about serious crimes, and nothing about illegal aliens and gangs. The result is a nanny state where the public is terrorized by street crime. And when the control mechanisms are in place, the door opens to hardcore repression. You should look it up."

"I'll read up on it. I agree, it makes me sick. I felt like a heel busting into your place, and all the other times. My attitude makes me unpopular with the top brass, of course. We somehow don't have resources to investigate real crime unless it's pretty drastic. What you did qualifies, so I propose we adjourn before anyone comes to check on their precious ROFLCOPTER, and continue this discussion later."

"I'll be looking forward to it. My fiancée will be very interested too; recent events have been an eye-opener."

"I should mention, there are some folks who are a bit disturbed by the way things have been going. We have, shall we say, a little club. The Resistance sure could use a talented fellow like you. We could make a pretty good team. What do you say?"

"Forward the Revolution!"

THE END

28 - Rainbow Albrecht

Rainbow Albrecht works diligently to enrich his multi-billionaire CEO. His tireless toil likewise helps keep several layers of management swimming in gravy. The pencil-pushing bureaucrats generously reward the people who actually get the job done by constantly creating new policies, microscopically scrutinizing them with database-driven metrics, and devising clever ways to reduce their pay.

When Rainbow is not serving his greedy corporate masters while plotting world domination, he writes stories, mostly humorous science fiction and fantasy. If you liked this story, please visit Rainbow's author page:
https://amazon.com/author/rainbowalbrecht

See my blog for updates:
https://rainbowalbrecht.wordpress.com/

For my right wing / reactionary / deplorable / meanie Fascist tirades on *Return of Kings*, see:
http://www.returnofkings.com/author/rainbowal brecht_rok